KISS WITH CHEMISTRY

CLOSE YOUR EYES & READ THE BOOK

NAGASAI GANGINENI

Made with ♥ on the Notion Press Platform
www.notionpress.com

For my dear....,

i @ you

You were really a great person , friend , and more ....,

I loves your happiness .

so I think we should just be forever my dear....@

ᑭᑭᑭ

Contents

Foreword

We have shared a lot of words , meals , deals and hoped around the world together .

That's all to say that , while I consider my self a good watcher and a hunter for love .

She is the one in people I call most for advice , and I be her in most habitats that make me

here to blow the air as Kiss , into the ballon as love ; with the eyes full of thirst......@nagasai344 .

Preface

It's been a long time coming, but this day , this hour tipped open a global outpouring for change, exposing some of the most insid- ious elements of the *Kiss with Chemistry* .

Love has a phase of thirst without the physical but their is a soul of love called Memories . #love, and the Dreams for Love with out being love is a control raised as the universal call against violence and domination. We are poised on a lust, but at its core, this is beyond Sex, Hugs, or Kiss.

Underneath the layers of Kiss in Love lies a profound imbalance between the You and Me .

WHAT IS KISS ?

Come on friends its not 90's its 20's and you all here to learn the Kiss.....hahaha !

If you were really here to know the Style of Kissing in World of Romance with the Thirst of Love.....Welcome to the

KISS WITH CHEMISTRY .

Even I dont know what is Kiss actually because I did not have my First Kiss till now....!

Everyday i realise that i was in a Dream its not real.....come on wake up.......@ But its ok...for everything that their is no one for me as a...

We all Love the Girls that are top scored in our Crush List . Some dare up and propose like me and even having the zero knowledge in it .....even all through days and months even it happens years I LOVE HER @

This Book is recomended that the Souls are in Love not in Lust .

KISS >

Kiss is a Alcoholic that keeps in the world of Romance in a Closed Room of Love .

When the souls have an Alcohol in reqiured state that brings the level of dirtymind . Every Kiss between the dirtymind is the memory forever which can control in your long releationship .

DirtyMind is not a bad state . Maintaining the level of State is Important .

Also not the bodies to hug but the souls need it . When you are in the level of state you will go to a world called Romance .

It most probabily decides , wheather you will enter the room of Love or not . Romance is the Kitchen of Dishes that only chef can play .

Yeah all have differet thought of approach......,*I Accept that , but Kiss is an art of emotion in many ways even the charm on face is enough for weighted hearts ....!*

@nagasai344

♡♡♡

WAR IN ROMANCE

Welcome back you friend , Its about 08 : 39 PM with a coffee holding in my hand and a Baby under my chest with Tight sleepy Hug with an Useless Conservation and the Sky says to Fullfill the Thirst & the Moon hides in to the sky like she hides in me & the breeze is finding us in the night .

After waking up I realised that , All good but its not real.......! I was on my bed even their is no Coffee for me.........!

Here I come to the topic of *WAR IN ROMANCE* , *Many Great Wars are with Closest Loved Ones........! yeah that's True .*

Here Wars means not the physical attack , Its a night with your Love , Watching the End of Titanic in a Room that you are Alone .... I say Sex is not a War its a Part of it .

While thinking the day of your life with your Love........,

Its True.......,

wait...,

A Question I have Got.......*

@nagasai344

"Will you still Love me ,If I won't be yours ? " She Asked !

I Replied " You were not mine when I fell Love with you , but i still did because I lost myself to you , So as far as that doesn't change , I will keep Loving you I guess ."

Its about 10 : 00 PM ,

Climate is trying to tell something .

The Moon Speaks with its Shine & The Stars running in the Sky and hiding on the clouds .

Do you observe the Moon speaks the language of Love , and the Stars is War on clouds ....WHAT A BEATUY .

Lets Tip for a small Challenge ::

Ok , Today We can Observe the Sky tonight ,with a peace of mind ...... Its trains you to Understand the Nature's Drama @love .

Music is the Loud voice for so many Quiet Hearts .

♡♡♡

RESPECT

Its time to heal all the pain ....,

Get ready for sure presence of Satisfaction With Heartfull of Love .

Life is unfair

You put someone first, who puts you second.. you give 110% to someone in a relationship who only gives 40%. you're there for a best friend at 3.01AM and the next day they don't pick up their phone. it seems like you're giving everyone everything and they're just walking away with it .

@ RESPECT IS ONE OF THE GREATEST EXPRESSION OF LOVE .

When a man says sorry for his mistake , Belive him and he's wise .

When a man says sorry for not his mistake , Belive me friend he will be one most heartfull person for the reason of you , And you will be cries for his presence .

Hurting to someone is easy as throwing a Stone in an Ocean , But you will never no how ***deep*** the Stone will go...,

One day in a Conservation my Friend Asked me ::

What is Love ?

As i said , It is a pain that offer you the values of small things in a great way . When you Stop Zooming the same picture and eyes hold the silent tears.....,

If i was a Child In School :: You are my Question ? , with a Formula of Love .

If i were in past :: You are a War , with a weapon of Love .

If i was an Scientist :: You were a Reaction for our Bond .

If i was an artist :: You were the Beauty of my Picture .

In Me :: It's you !

Every day the night have a seperate Fan base......I was the one who tired up for the person without a reason .

You deserve to fall in love with someone who loves all of you . Someone who falls in to you . Someone who can see the value in Communication is the time for Healing in Expression .

Someone who embodies the defination of Acceptence is the Essence of Connection . Someone who is Emotionally invested the your Love in the Bank of a Girl and Intentinally present . Someone who can provide the sense of safty is an Emotion in Trust .

Respect is a Journey with Different types of Souls with many Stories........., some becomes Accendentally Hurt and some with the reason .

Respect the person with no reason & Love the person like you ::
@nagasai344

ღღღ

LOVE WITH/WITHOUT KISS

Begining this era may hoping the night with the ruin of stars calling the clouds to cover the eyes of moon in between you and me .

You know , what the day tells to the night having the same clear sky like you is I LOVE YOU >3 .

When you feel sad , you can come to me .

I'll Listen .

I'll Never turn you away .

I hear you .

Even when you don't have word to say.....@Iam here .

#if you are alone , I will be your shadow in the night .

#if you want to cry , I will be your shoulder with a folding reason of tears for me .

#if you were not happy , I will make my smile for you .

#if you need me at time , I will be time for you in the times of even or odd .

Change is the only constant in life, and resisting it is like trying to hold back the tide with your hands. You may be able to keep hold of a small amount of water for a short while, but you'll be too afraid to move in case you spill any, and you'll be so focused on what's in your hands that you will miss what the new tide brings.

Love & friendship are beautiful, but they are even more beautiful 'when you find them in the same person. When you have someone who understands you, supports you, who makes you laugh, and who is always there for you. You have someone who you can share your hopes and dreams, your fears and doubts, your joys and sorrows. You have someone who you can rely on, who you can trust, and who you can love with all your heart .

How Do I Kiss

For the Uninvited Guest in the party of my Life.....,

One day i will say that ***Iam Completly in Love with you .***

Kiss her slowly , take your own time, Kiss her like you have forgotten the world you be & be the flavour you have ever touched for an expression of Kiss .

Kiss her with a Curious childish delight .

Laugh in to her soul , inhale her sighs .

Kiss her until she moans .

Kiss her with her face in your hands .

Or your hands playing with her hair .

And pulling her close to the Waist .

Kiss her like she's the brightest thing you have ever seen .

Take your Time Kiss her like the First and only peice of Chocolate that you die for the taste of it .

Kiss her in the way that she never not want to kiss anyone else ever agian .

♡♡♡

The Last Word For You

A Word of Communication that are found for no reason in Your Last Word .

Comment the Feelings that felt you to come to the end of this book.....in another word THE BEGINING .

Your words of feeling ::

>>>>>>

www.ingramcontent.com/pod-product-compliance
Ingram Content Group UK Ltd.
Pitfield, Milton Keynes, MK11 3LW, UK
UKHW041846200726
13854UKWH00005BA/2236

9 798889 517573